Not Friends

Rebecca Bender

pajama press

Canada Council Conseil des arts
for the Arts du Canada

ONTARIO ARTS COUNCIL
CONSEIL DES ARTS DE L'ONTARIO
an Ontario government agency
un organisme du gouvernement de l'Ontario

Canadä

The publisher gratefully acknowledges the support of the Canada Council for the Arts and the Ontario Arts Council for its publishing program. We acknowledge the financial support of the Government of Canada through the Canada Book Fund (CBF) for our publishing activities.

Publisher Cataloging-in-Publication Data (U.S.)

Names: Bender, Rebecca, 1980-, author.
Title: Not Friends / Rebecca Bender.
Description: Toronto, Ontario Canada : Pajama Press, 2017. | Summary: "Giraffe and Bird are not friends. After all, they bicker all the time. But when they go their separate ways and a scary storm strikes, they both realize they might be better off together—even if they are still *not* friends" -- Provided by publisher.
Identifiers: ISBN 978-1-77278-026-0 (hardcover)
Subjects: LCSH: Giraffe – Juvenile fiction. | Birds – Juvenile fiction. | Friendship – Juvenile fiction. | BISAC: JUVENILE FICTION / Social Themes / Friendship.
Classification: LCC PZ7.B464Not |DDC [E] – dc23

Manufactured by Qualibre Inc. / Print Plus
Printed in China

Cover and book design—Rebecca Bender

Pajama Press Inc.
181 Carlaw Ave. Suite 207 Toronto, Ontario Canada, M4M 2S1

Distributed in the U.S. by Ingram Publisher Services
1 Ingram Blvd. La Vergne, TN 37086, USA

Original art created with acrylic paint on texturized illustration board.

For all the little birds in my life

It's true that **getting along** can be difficult.
If the bird could tell you, he'd say
he **can't stand** the giraffe.

And if the giraffe could tell you, he'd say
he **can't abide** the bird.

The bird, you see, makes funny faces at the giraffe.

And the giraffe sticks out his **long tongue** at the bird.

This makes the bird **twitter** in the giraffe's ear.

Tweet!

Tweet!

Tweet!

That makes the giraffe **invade** the bird's personal space.

Some days the giraffe has **bad breath.**

Other days the bird eats
too many berries
(which are high in fiber).

Frequently the giraffe makes loud noises when he **chews** his food with his **mouth open.**

Often the bird **slurps** up a **slimy worm** in front of the giraffe.

Sometimes the bird **prunes** his feathers just above the giraffe's head.

sniffle

sniffle

This makes the giraffe sneeze.

Every time the giraffe lets out a sneeze,
the bird is **blown right off**
the telephone wire.

W!

Flap
Flap
Flap

And every time the bird is blown off the telephone wire, he flies up to **perch right on** the giraffe's horns.

When the bird perches on the giraffe's horns,
the giraffe **swats** him with his ears.

When the giraffe swats the bird with his ears,
the bird **pecks** him with his beak.

The pecking makes the giraffe shake his head until they are **both dizzy.**

Dizzy and woozy, they **both tumble** to the ground.

One day, the giraffe loses his patience and shouts at the bird,

The bird gets fed up and shouts back at the giraffe,

Get lost, Giraffe!

So they do.

That night, there is a seriously scary storm.
All the telephone poles crash to the ground.

The giraffe wishes he could hide his eyes under
the bird's feathers so he wouldn't see the lightning.
The bird wishes he could hide under
the giraffe's ears so he wouldn't hear the thunder.

CRACK!

BOOM!

BANG!

The next morning, the bird feels **glum**. He has nowhere to sit, and no one to **pick** and **peck**.

The giraffe feels lonely. There is no one around
to pester and perturb him.

With no one around to pester him,
the giraffe has time to think.
The funny thing is that all the giraffe can
can think about is the bird.

What can he do
to bring the bird back?

The giraffe agrees to help
the **telephone company** for a while.

He doesn't have to wait long for the bird to return.
He also doesn't have to wait long for the bird to
start **making faces again.**

Now it's true that getting along can be difficult.
And if you asked these two, the giraffe might still say
he **can't abide** the bird,